Flying Low

Alain M. Bergeron

illustrated by
Sampar

translated by
Marie-Michèle Gingras

Scholastic Canada Ltd.

Toronto New York London Auckland Sydney
Mexico City New Delhi Hong Kong Buenos Aires

Scholastic Canada Ltd.
604 King Street West, Toronto, Ontario M5V 1E1, Canada

Scholastic Inc.
557 Broadway, New York, NY 10012, USA

Scholastic Australia Pty Limited
PO Box 579, Gosford, NSW 2250, Australia

Scholastic New Zealand Limited
Private Bag 94407, Botany, Manukau 2163, New Zealand

Scholastic Children's Books
Euston House, 24 Eversholt Street, London NW1 1DB, UK

Library and Archives Canada Cataloguing in Publication

Bergeron, Alain M., 1957-

Flying low / by Alain M. Bergeron ; illustrations by Sampar ;
translation by Marie-Michèle Gingras.

Originally published under title: Zzzut!: un roman.
ISBN 978-1-4431-1392-2

1. Abel, Dominic (Fictitious character)--Juvenile fiction.
I. Sampar II. Gingras, Marie-Michèle III. Title.

PS8553.E67454Z4713   2012jC843'.54   C2012-901649-7

6 5 4 3 2 1   Printed in Canada 121   12 13 14 15 16

*for my friend
Samuel Parent
— A.M.B.*

Chapter 1
Ready for Anything . . . Well, Almost

I am so ready.

Today we are doing our oral presentations in school.

I have to go first. That's because of my last name — Abel.

I don't mind going first. I get a little stressed out. But I like to get it out of the way.

1

Once it's over, I can relax.

I wouldn't want my friend Anthony's last name. It's Vernon. That means he's the last one to go — except when Ms. Allison starts at the end of our class list. That drives me crazy, because then *I'm* the last one up. It takes forever for my turn to come. I just sit there getting more and more freaked out.

If you think oral presentations are boring, then you should be in my class.

For our last presentation we got to bring in our pets for show and tell. Sophie brought her hamster and it escaped from its cage. We tore the classroom apart looking for it.

It was in the perfect hiding spot under Ms. Allison's desk. We never would have found it.

But then Charles's cat, Tiger, got loose, too!

It didn't take long for Tiger to sniff out the hamster. It's amazing how fast a cat can move when it's hungry.

Sophie told Charles that her *next* pet would be a dog — a huge dog. Like a Doberman!

All of that was nothing compared to what Anthony's frog did to Emma's bug collection.

For today's presentation, we have to talk about the most amazing day we ever had.

That's easy.

The most amazing day of my life was the day my little sister, Isabelle, was born.

I was so happy when my parents brought her home. I almost cried. Good thing I didn't — Isabelle cried enough for both of us. But I thought she was perfect.

My mom helped me write my speech about Isabelle. We read it together twice. Then she taught me a trick. A mymomic device . . . ? No, I think it was a mnemonic device.

Anyway, the trick is to do little drawings to help remember the words. I drew a diaper to help me remember Isabelle.

I read my speech twice using my mom's trick. The third time I said it from memory. I didn't need to look at my paper at all!

That night I fell asleep with my speech
under my pillow. When I woke up the next
morning, a quick look at my paper was all
it took. I still remembered the whole thing
without reading it.

And now the day of the presentation is
here at last. I'm a little nervous. But I know
my speech so well. What could go wrong?

The presentations start after recess, and I can't wait.

The bell rings to go outside. I race for the door.

Oh, wait. I think I need to make a pit stop — too much orange juice this morning. I head for the washroom.

"Are you coming, Dom?" Anthony yells after me.

Dom is my nickname — it's short for Dominic.

"I'll meet you out there," I say. I run into the boys' room.

There's a lot of echo in the washroom, *washroom, washroom* . . . My voice echoes much better in here than in the one at home.

You hear all sorts of strange and funny noises in here. I wonder if it's the same in the girls' washroom.

Sometimes I like to play with the echo. But some days it really stinks in here! That's when I get in and out quickly.

Today I go into the stall and undo my pants. I take aim and hit my target. Bull's eye! I start to go over my presentation in my head.

I finish and flush the toilet. It roars like it wants to swallow me!

"Thank you for your attention," I say as I finish my speech. I'd remembered it perfectly.

I am so ready for my presentation. Everything is going just the way I planned. I'm going to ace this. Except . . .

Uh-oh! I'm stuck!

Chapter 2
A Small Problem

I have a small problem.

A small, but very important problem.

The zipper on my pants is stuck at the bottom.

I tug it gently. Stuck.

I tug it hard. Stuck.

No matter how much I pull, nothing

moves. I'm not worried. It's actually kind of funny. What a dumb thing to happen.

I pull again. Nothing.

I just want my zipper up so I can go outside and play soccer with my friends. If I go out with my fly open, everyone will laugh at me!

I take a deep breath and think. What if I try using my left hand? My right hand is stronger. But maybe pulling it from another side will help. It's worth a try.

I take the zipper in my left hand . . . The elevator is getting ready to go up . . .

Oh, no!

The elevator's out of order and the door is stuck.

And it's not like I can take the stairs.

Okay, they say that what goes up must come down. The opposite might be true, right?

I tug again.

I guess not.

I don't find this very funny anymore. Plus, it's hot in this stall. Sweat is rolling down my forehead.

I wipe it using some toilet paper. It feels like sandpaper, then it falls apart. Why does our school always go for the cheap stuff?

I take a deep breath and grip my zipper with both hands. This is going to be it.

One, two, three . . . Go! I pull with all my might.

It's moved! Yes, it's moved one tiny notch.
Only forty more to go.

Okay, time to try for another notch, maybe two. I pull and I pull and . . .

Nothing.

It's useless. Has it been glued there?

These are brand new pants — I want my money back!

Chapter 3
Recess Is Over

I have to get out of here.

What if I run home to change my pants? If I'm fast, maybe I can make it back in time for my presentation.

But I'll have to go to the office and ask for permission first.

Riiiinnng!

The bell! It's too late.

Recess is over.

I hear everyone coming in.

Which means that I have to go back to class, too. With my zipper open.

No!

There is no way I am moving from this spot. No way am I going to show up in Ms. Allison's class with my barn door open. Especially since I'm wearing my SpongeBob boxers — super flashy *and* neon yellow!

I have to come up with a plan! What if I walk into my classroom and try to make eye contact with everyone? No. Then it would just be easier to see them looking down at my pants. Though I bet just the girls would be looking. The boys would be too busy laughing to stare.

My friend Charles wouldn't care if he were

in my place. He would do his presentation in a bathing suit if it got him extra marks. He doesn't care what people think. I'm different. I'd never remember my speech with everyone staring!

What if I cover my barn door using the paper with my speech on it? Ms. Allison probably wouldn't let me hold it, though. We're supposed to know our speech by heart. There's another idea down the toilet . . .

If I'd brought my baseball cap to school, I could have covered myself. Maybe I can borrow one! No, that won't work. Hats aren't allowed inside the classroom.

Covering up my fly wouldn't help, anyway. I move my arms too much when I'm presenting. Ms. Allison likes it when we do that.

Plus, when I say that I love my sister Isabelle "*thiiis much*," I open my arms really wide. People would see *everything*!

What if I turn my back to the class and talk directly to the board? Would I get points for originality?

No, I'd probably just lose points for not making eye contact.

I have it!

All I have to do is leave my shirt untucked. Then I'll pull it down as much as I can. So smart! A jammed zipper can't stop me!

Oh. Too bad for me my shirt is too short to hide my . . . well, you know.

What if I take off my shirt and then tuck it into my pants? No, I'm too skinny — everyone will see that I don't have big muscles. What if they started counting my ribs?

What I really need is a big storm to come along and knock out the power. That would work! In the dark, no one would notice my wardrobe malfunction. If only it weren't so sunny out.

Why couldn't I catch the chicken pox?

Chapter 4
A Little Help

I'm trapped. I feel like a rat in cage. Are the walls starting to close in around me? I'm losing it.

Deep breath.

It doesn't help that I know my classmates must be in their chairs by now. Ms. Allison is getting ready to call the first name . . .

"Dom?"

Anthony! He's come to help! He'll know what to do.

"In here!" I shout.

Underneath the door, two running shoes appear.

"Are you sick, Dom? What's taking so long?"

"No, I am not sick."

"What are you doing? Ms. Allison is looking for you everywhere. Is the door jammed?"

Anthony bangs on the door three times. It rattles and the sound echoes through the washroom.

"It's not the door . . ."

"What is it, then?" asks Anthony.

"Well . . ." I'm embarrassed.

Should I tell him about it? It's not as if I have a choice.

I mutter, "My zipper is broken."

"What?"

"My zipper. I can't close it!"

I wait for an answer. It's taking a little too long to come.

"Anthony? Are you still there?"

"Ye . . . Ye . . . yes. *Mmmph!*"

And then he bursts out into loud laughter that fills the entire washroom.

"Haaaaa! Ha! Ha! Ha!" he splutters.

I'm not enjoying the echo now.

It's my turn to bang on the door.

"Hey! This is serious! I'm stuck in here! I'm . . . stalled!" I shout. Anthony's not really the help I thought he'd be.

Silence again.

"Sss . . . stalled in the toilet stall!"

Another burst of laughter. Just as bad as the first one.

"Stop!" he says. "I'm going to wet my pants."

Which wouldn't be a bad thing. Then he'd be stuck in here, too!

Anthony gets in the stall next to mine. He pees for a long time — what did *he* drink this morning? He finally flushes the toilet and gets out.

I see his running shoes back in front of my door.

"Do you want some help?"

"Yeah. What would you do if you were me?"

"I know — firefighters! Like when your tongue got stuck on the pole last winter. I'll call 4-1-1!"

"It's 9-1-1, and *no*!" I could see the headlines now: *Boy, Flying Low, Rescued. Story on page 8.*

I sigh. "Why don't you just go get the school principal for me?"

"Good idea. He'll know what to do. I'll be right back."

I hear him walk away. Before he leaves, he calls, "Stay there . . ." I can hear his laughter ring out in the hall.

Would it be this funny if it were *his* zipper? I don't think so.

Still, I'm lucky it's not photo day. I'm not very tall. I'd be seated in the front row for sure. *Say cheese!* Could you imagine if it got in the yearbook?

To kill time, I start flushing the toilet. I watch it as it flows down — the water spins. I heard that in Australia it spins the other way. I should ask Ms. Allison if that's true.

Four flushes later, Anthony comes back with help.

"Dom? Mr. Seater was out, but Mrs. Morgan, the secretary, is here."

I see her shoes under the door. It's her turn to knock.

"Doom— I mean, Dominic! Do you need a hand?" asks Mrs. Morgan.

"No! Um, thanks. Hey, Anthony, stop laughing!"

Mrs. Morgan is a really nice person. But she's a girl. Old — even as old as my mom — but still, she's a *girl*.

I hear a knock. Then a new voice enters the room.

"Anthony? Have you found Dominic?"

Oh, no! It's Ms. Allison! Don't these people know this is the *boys'* washroom?

"Dom, you have another vi-si-tor," says Anthony. He bangs once on the door for each syllable.

Could this get anymore embarrassing?

More knocks. This time from Ms. Allison!

"Dominic? Come out of there!" she orders.

"I can't! And please, stop banging on the door!"

"What's going on?" asks Ms. Allison.

"I—I'm not ready for my presentation."

I'd rather lie than tell her the truth.

I hear whispers. Just like when Anthony

whispers answers in my ear in class. Then I hear quiet giggles. Ms. Allison can't hold back her laughter!

Here I am having the worst day ever, and on other side of the door they're having a party! I guess that makes me the clown.

I'm feeling pretty sorry for myself. But at least it can't get any worse.

Then I hear the washroom door open once again . . .

Chapter 5
A Delicate,
But Not Quite Desperate, Situation

Before I know it, my entire class is in the washroom! They're running around everywhere. Some of the girls start to point out strange things.

"Hey, what are these white candies doing in these bowls?"

It's Emma's voice.

Anthony tells her that those are little mints. He says that she can taste one if she wants. Luckily, Ms. Allison stops her before she can try one.

Everyone's asking what's going on. It doesn't take long for Anthony to proudly tell them.

My pride is at stake here, and what are they doing? Laughing. A lot.

If I could flush myself down the toilet and disappear, I would.

How can I ever face them again?

I'm doomed to spend the rest of my days in a toilet stall. My meals will have to be slid under my door, like a prisoner's. This is where I will eat, drink, sleep sitting down, wash, grow old and die. My ashes will be thrown into the bowl. As the toilet is flushed, they'll sing: *Amazing Grace, how sweet the sound . . .*

Ms. Allison asks everyone to please be quiet. She tries to convince me to open the door.

"Come on, Dominic. Enough of this. It's time to come out."

"No way," Anthony says, laughing. "We already had the *Show* and *Tell* presentation!"

Once again the washroom echoes with laughter. I owe him for that.

"Hey, Ms. Allison, what if I lend him my pants? I could switch places with him and wait for him to come back . . ."

It's Xavier Bowen. I recognize his squeaky voice. He'd do anything to put off talking in front of the class. He hates oral presentations. He comes right after me on the class list: Abel, then Bowen.

We don't wear the same size pants at all — he's much taller and wider. I'd look silly in his pants. I'd still get laughed at — just for a different reason.

But there's no way Ms. Allison is going to fall for his offer. "That's very generous of you, Xavier," she says. "But that won't stop you from doing your presentation."

"Yes, but Ms. Allison, like I said before, Xavier is actually my last name. Bowen is my first name. They made a mistake on my birth certificate."

"After the letter A comes the letter B — as in Bowen! End of discussion!" declares my teacher.

"It's too bad, Ms. Allison," I say through the door. "Because I really was ready to go first."

"I have an idea, Dominic," says Ms. Allison. "What if you did your presentation from there?"

"With the door closed?"

"Well, yes," answers Ms. Allison. "It might be too distracting otherwise."

Brilliant! Why didn't I think of that?

"Let's do it!" I shout.

I imagine myself in front of the class. With my zipper up, of course. I picture the other students sitting down, well-behaved. I quickly go over my mymomic device . . . the mnemonic . . . the trick my mother taught me. I picture the diaper and it all comes back to me.

"Hello," I start. "Today I will tell you about the most amazing day of my life. Obviously, it's not today." (I have just come up with that part.)

"The most amazing day of my life was when my baby sister, Isabelle, came home from the hospital. Her skin was all pink and new. She didn't have any teeth or hair yet. But she was still beautiful.

"My parents let me hold her in my arms. It made my muscles look big. They put her crib in my room. I had to move to the basement, so I could sleep at night — unlike my mom. When Isabelle was first born, she was up all night! I like having my room in the basement. I love my Isabelle this much—"

Bang!

My hands have hit the walls on the sides of the toilet stall. I was stretching my arms to show how much I love my sister.

"Thank you for your attention."

There! I nailed it. Just like I'd planned. Well, almost . . .

To my surprise, my classmates start to clap. I'm so happy, I forget where I am. I bend over to take a bow. Because that was part of my plan.

Bang!

I've whacked my forehead on the stall door. Ouch!

That was stupid. Nobody can even see me!

"Good work, Dominic," says Ms. Allison. "Now . . . You'll have to get out of there . . . at some point."

"Excuse me, but what are you all doing in here?" I recognize the deep voice of the school janitor, Mr. Robertson.

Ms. Allison quietly tells him about the situation.

"I see . . . I see . . ." he says. He doesn't laugh. Here's a man who understands!

"I've got just the thing. I'll be right back," he says.

A moment later his work shoes show up under my door. He reaches over and hands me a plain old pencil.

"Use this on your zipper," he says. "Draw on both sides, and everything should go back to normal."

I follow his instructions. I'm very careful not to draw on my pants. The last thing I need is a big mark on the front of them!

I take a deep breath. I start pulling the zipper up. It glides to the top.

I'm so happy, I cheer!

Holding up the pencil, I open the door. Freedom!

I feel like I've just been released from prison.

At first everyone looks at my zipper.

Awkward.

But soon I'm welcomed by a bunch of

"Hoorays!" and "Congrats!" Now everyone is smiling at me.

I give the magic pencil back to Mr. Robertson. I can't thank him enough!

"Ms. Allison, it's my turn!" Xavier Bowen suddenly shouts. Everyone is shocked.

We watch as Xavier locks himself up in the toilet stall and starts his presentation.

"Hello. I am going to tell you about the most amazing day of my life . . ."

And on that day, for the first and only time in the history of Leslie Nielson Public School, the boys' washroom became a classroom.

The echo really added something to the presentations!

Epilogue
Not Again!

When I get home at lunchtime, I kiss Isabelle. Then I tell my parents about my horrible morning. We all laugh, including me. It's funny now. Mostly.

Just before I leave to go back to school, I head to the washroom. I had a lot of milk at lunch.

"Uh-oh! Not again!" I shout.

"What is it, honey?" asks my mom from the kitchen.

"It's my zipper!"

"Is it stuck again?"

"Yes, but now it won't come down!" I start to do a little dance. It's almost like a rain dance. Because if I don't get these pants off soon, there could be some rain!

Alain M. Bergeron

I can't honestly say that the memories I have of my oral presentations are very good ones. In fact, I'm just starting to recover from them!

Back then, the idea of having to talk in front of a room full of students was terrifying to me — even if they were my friends. And despite the fact that I wrote my speech in advance, and practised, and practised again, I would always forget everything as soon as my teacher called my name. And when your last name is Bergeron, your turn comes up really quickly.

It felt like I was stuck in the middle of a forest and I couldn't get out of the words — I mean the woods. And as I was quite shy, I never really knew how to stand and talk in front of a group. It was a nightmare every single time!

When I was done, I went back to my seat. In fact, I ran back. Then I did what everyone else did: I made fun of the boys and girls who came after me.

Samuel Parent

Because my last name is not Abel or Zohnson, but Parent, I was always pretty much in the middle of the pack when the teacher asked us to go up and do an oral presentation. Each time I heard my name, my heart started to beat really fast. I would glance at my sheet one more time, and then

I became the class's target.

I'd get up to the front, ready to go.

Sort of.

I would try to visualize my sheet of paper — which was now kilometres away from me, on my desk. The only line that I could think of was, "Thank you for your attention."

Great — all I could remember was the last line of my speech! I was not a very talented speaker at the time . . . and I haven't improved much since.

Oral presentations? No thanks. I would much rather illustrate ideas in children's books.

Thank you for your attention . . .